Dad's Runaway BUTT!

Dawn McMillan

Illustrated by Ross Kinnaird

Dover Publications
Garden City, New York

Dad's butt has

blown off!

With a *hiss* and a **roar**
 it's gone out our front door ...

Way down our walk, out through the gate.

"Let's *chase* it, Dad, before it's too late!"

What a disaster! His butt's rolling **faster!**
Off down the street past people we meet.

It **toots** and it **blows!** I hold my nose!

As it's ...

Rolling and rolling, past people strolling.

Past joggers in tights.

Past bikers with lights.

Past children **swinging**.

Past people **singing**.

Uphill and down, heading for town.

My heart is racing from *running* and *chasing!*

And now ...

the police have arrived!
They shout,
"Stand aside! We're coming through!"

"This butt on the **loose** will never do!
Not to mention it's a **smelly butt** too!"

"This butt causes crashes, bad falls …

and splashes.

"And with that smell on the breeze,

it's **wilting** the trees."

The police are shouting, **"We're on its tail!**
We'll have to ARREST it and take it to jail.
We'll catch this bad butt by the end of the day.
A runaway butt is never okay!"

Yet ...

Dad needs his butt!
So what happens now?
We **must** get his butt back.
The question is,
"How?"

My heart is **HEAVY**. I'm feeling **sad**.
I don't want
a butt-free Dad.

Now Dad's getting tired.
He's done with the chase.
He's heading home
with a frown on his face.

But wait ...

What do I see? Can it be right?

I smell a smell and ...

Dad's butt is in **sight!**
It's **rolled** around the block.
It's out on its own!
Now it's **chasing** Dad
and we're heading for home!

And **abracadabra!**
Dad's butt's back in place!
Now he's in one piece,
with a **smile** on his face!

We're a family united
And I'm so excited!
No more butt scurries!
No more butt worries.

I give Dad a hug and I say ...

"Dad, please ..."

About the author

Hi, I'm Dawn McMillan. I'm from Waiomu, a small coastal village on the western side of the Coromandel Peninsula in New Zealand. I live with my husband, Derek, and our cat, Joyce. I write some sensible stories and lots of crazy stories! I love creating quirky characters and hope you enjoy reading about them.

About the illustrator

Hi, I'm Ross. I love to draw. When I'm not drawing, or being cross with my computer, I love most things involving the sea and nature. I also work from a little studio in my garden surrounded by birds and trees. I live in Auckland, New Zealand. I hope you like reading this book as much as I enjoyed illustrating it.

This Dover edition, first published in 2024, is an unabridged republication of the work published as *My Dad's Runaway BUM!* by Oratia Media Ltd., Auckland, New Zealand, in 2024. The text has been Americanized for this edition.

ISBN-13: 978-0-486-85317-8
ISBN-10: 0-486-85317-9

Manufactured in the United States of America
85317901   2024
www.doverpublications.com